WHAT ON EARTH?

Wood

BART AND LYNN KING

High Noon Books
Novato, California

Editor: Deb Akers
Interior Illustrations: Cynthia Coverston
Cover Design: Bonni Gatter

International Standard Book Number: 978-1-57128-433-4

16 15 14 13 12 11 10 09 08 07
10 09 08 07 06 05 04 03 02 01

Contents

CHAPTER 1

Wood on Wheels

Val put her right foot on her skateboard. Then she pushed off of the ground with her left foot. Val picked up speed. She started to glide down a small hill. Three of her pals were down the hill. She wanted to sneak up on them. Val crouched down on her skateboard as it rolled.

"Where do you think she is?" asked Nate. He, Tess, and Sam were waiting for Val. They were in front of a skateboard shop. Val had told them to meet there.

1

Just then, Val went past in a blur. She headed right for a bench. In the blink of an eye, she turned hard and missed the bench.

"Val has skills on that board," said Sam.

The group watched Val skate along a curb. Then they heard a loud CRACK. Val fell down. Her skateboard broke into two pieces. The three ran up to Val.

"Are you OK?" asked Tess.

Val nodded and stood. "I am OK, but my skateboard is not," she said. Sam and Nate handed her the broken parts of her board.

"At least you picked a good place to break your board," said Sam. They all looked at the skateboard shop. Val stretched and rubbed her

Her skateboard broke into two pieces.

back. It hurt a bit.

"Yes," said Val. "Today must be my lucky day." She rolled her eyes. Then she headed into the shop. It was full of kids looking for the perfect skateboard.

Val gave the broken board to a worker. Val said she wanted a new skateboard deck. But she wanted her old wheels on the new deck.

The worker showed Val a wall. On it were lots of plain skateboard decks. There were many different shapes and sizes. They were made of a hard, light brown wood. The boards were light in weight.

"Val's skateboard was made of wood?" asked Tess.

Nate was shocked, too. The old board had all kinds of stickers and tape. It was hard to tell what it was made of!

"Wood is used for lots of sports stuff," said Sam. "Like for baseball bats."

"And boats and oars," said Nate.

"Or the heads of golf clubs," said Tess.

Val picked a new deck. Then she made plans to come back to the shop. She would pick up her new board then. She walked up to her pals.

"Hey, Val," said Sam. "I love that trick where you break your skateboard!"

"Very funny, Sam," said Val. She gave Sam a punch in the arm.

5

Tess turned to Val. She said she had not known that skateboards were still made of wood.

"They sure are," Val said. "The best ones are made of wood. Wood is all around us."

The four of them looked up all at once.

"I just got a thought for our next film," said Tess. "What if we did it on wood?"

They took a film class taught by Ms. Reese. The class worked in groups. The four pals had made a team.

"I like it," said Val. "But this time I want to do the filming."

"That is my job!" said Sam.

Nate held up his hand. "I think we should

share the work," he said. He gave Val a wink. "But if Sam can pass this quiz, then he can still film."

Val gave a nod.

"Ask away," said Sam.

"How does wood keep us warm *and* cool?" asked Nate.

"Easy," said Sam. "To keep warm, you can start a fire with wood. Or you can make a house with it."

"And how can wood keep you cool?" asked Nate.

Sam thought and thought. But he could not come up with anything.

"I give up," Sam said at last.

"If you are too warm, you can stand in the shade of a tree to cool off," said Nate with a smile.

CHAPTER 2

Stumped

Val looked at Nate's back as they hiked down the trail. He was wearing a backpack with bottles of water for the two of them.

"Can you slow down?" Val asked. "I might miss some good stuff to film. And besides, I am getting tired."

Nate stopped and turned. He was glad they were making a film about wood. And the forest was the best place to start. That way they could film how all wood started. As a tree!

"This is as good a spot as any," Nate said. He waved his arm around them. "There is a lot of wood here. And it is living and growing."

"That is why they call it the WOODS," said Val. She looked into the lens. "Let's go off the trail a little. Then we can see more trees. I want to get the best ones on film."

Nate led the way. He brought Val to a spot where the trees were thick. Val got some of the trees on film.

"How do you know your way around so well?" Val asked.

"I come here to groom trails," Nate said. Grooming meant that Nate helped keep the trails open. He cleared them of twigs. He helped mark paths. That way, those who hiked could find their way. "I also save trees," Nate said. Val wanted to know what this meant, too.

Nate showed Val a green vine. It was curling around a tree.

"This vine should not grow here," Nate said. "It was brought here from far away. But the plant started to spread. If we do not pull it up, the vine can choke the life from trees! So I save trees by pulling up these vines."

Nate reached out to pull the vine.

"Hey, look at that!" Val said. She pointed to the sawed stump of a tree.

Nate let go of the vine. He went over and kneeled next to the stump. He looked at it closely. "Someone cut a tree down here," he said. "Maybe it was rotten or was not safe."

Then Nate and Val looked around. There were a lot of stumps in this part of the woods.

"Why are just some of the trees cut down?" said Nate. His voice sounded upset.

"I don't know," said Val. "But getting mad will not help."

"The way these trees are cut seems wrong to me," said Nate. The two had walked around a bit more. The stumps showed up here and there. It seemed like someone had done the cutting in a sneaky way. It was odd how only some trees had been cut. What if he and Val had not gone off the trail? They would not have seen the missing trees at all!

"Be sure to get some of these stumps on film," Nate said. "I think someone might be breaking the law here."

CHAPTER 3

A Chip off the Old Block

It was the next day. The four pals were at school. Nate and Val told Tess and Sam about the stumps in the woods. Tess and Sam thought it seemed odd, too. But the team needed more facts. Then they could think about what to do.

Also, they still had to work on the film. Nate and Val went to the library to learn more. Nate would look for Web sites. Val wanted to look for books.

"What should we do?" asked Sam.

Tess knew what to do. "Our film is on wood. Why don't we go see Mr. Holz in the wood shop?"

Sam and Tess started to walk to the class where Mr. Holz taught. They took a shortcut near the gym. They could tell the wood shop was near. The air was filled with the roar of saws. They could smell cut wood. The two walked into the wood shop. Mr. Holz was helping a girl make a bookcase.

"Hi, Mr. Holz," said Tess.

Mr. Holz looked up. "Hi, Tess. Hi, Sam," he said. "You two don't have my class today!"

"I know," Tess said. "But Sam and I are working on a film about wood. We thought you

15

could give us some tips."

Mr. Holz was glad to help. But first he had Tess and Sam put on shop glasses. It would keep their eyes safe.

"So, you are here to see me about wood," said Mr. Holz. "You did not have to come to wood shop for that."

Sam and Tess looked at him. "What do you mean?" asked Sam.

"Tess is taking notes. What is she writing on?" asked Mr. Holz.

Tess was writing on a white pad. "You are right," she said. "Each page of this pad comes from wood!"

"So does that stick you are writing with,"

16

said Mr. Holz with a wink. "Where else have you seen wood today?"

"The gym floor," said Sam. "And the seats in the stands."

"The classroom desks," said Tess.

Mr. Holz nodded. "Wood is all around. Keep your eyes open for it. There is also hidden wood."

"Hidden?" Sam and Tess both looked at Mr. Holz.

"Most houses are built of wood," said Mr. Holz. "You just can not see it inside the walls."

Sam and Tess thanked Mr. Holz and left. Next, they peeked in on Mrs. Roble. Mrs. Roble taught art.

A boy was painting one side of a wood block. Then he pressed the block on a large sheet from a pad.

Just then, Mrs. Roble, saw them. "Come look!" she said with a wave. She showed Sam and Tess what the class was working on. It was something called woodblock prints. A block of wood was carved on one side. The carved part was painted with ink. Then the carved wood was pressed onto a sheet of paper.

"Is it hard to carve wood?" asked Tess.

"There are two kinds of wood," said Mrs. Roble. "There is hard wood and soft wood. We use pine for our blocks. Pine is a soft wood. It is not hard to carve."

Sam knocked on one of the blocks. "This is soft?" he asked.

Mrs. Roble laughed. "Even soft wood is pretty hard. But hard wood can be nearly as hard as steel."

The boy they had been watching was now done. He showed them his print. It was an outdoor scene with trees by a lake.

Tess and Sam said it was a great picture.

"I think my grand dad made wood block prints," Sam said to Mrs. Roble. "Mom and Dad have some of the prints in frames. They are hanging on the wall in my room. Now I know how he made them."

"Then you should take this class," said

Mrs. Roble with a smile. "You may be a chip

off the old block!"

CHAPTER 4

Wood Wheels and Flying Boats

Val and Nate were finding out a lot about wood. Val had a stack of books. Nate was looking at Web sites.

"Wood helps us get from one place to the next," Val said.

"You mean it is not just for skateboards?" teased Nate.

Val made a face. "My skateboard has rubber wheels. But the first wheels ever made were wood." Val shared more. She had learned that folks wore wood shoes, wood ships sailed the seas, and horses pulled wood carts. "And wood planes fly in the sky!" she said.

Nate was shocked. "Wood planes?" he asked.

Val looked up from her book. "The biggest seaplane ever made was wood. It was called the Flying Boat. It took off and landed on the sea. And it could hold over 750 people, or two army tanks!"

"For real? How big was it?" Nate asked.

"The Flying Boat's wings were over 300 feet wide," said Val. "That's longer than a football field. And the book says it was five stories tall."

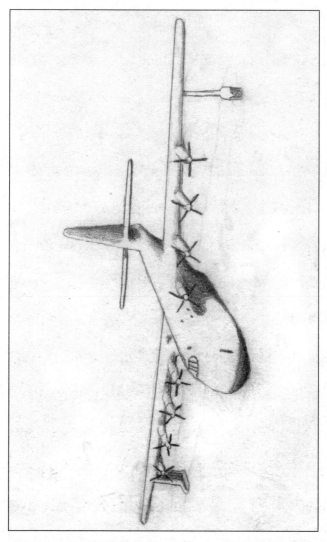

The biggest seaplane ever made was wood. It was called the Flying Boat.

"What kind of wood did they use? It had to be pretty strong," said Nate.

"It was mostly birch wood," said Val. "But it was nicknamed the Spruce Goose."

"That sounds better than the Birch Perch," said Nate.

Nate was looking at a Web site that taught about trees. The site said the U.S. cuts down and ships more trees than most places. And most of that wood goes into making houses. He told Tess about the Web site.

It said there are only so many trees out there. And more trees are cut down than can grow back. That is why there are laws for trees. The law says that only so many trees can be cut down in one place.

"Check this out," said Nate. "Most of the time, loggers clear cut. That means they cut down all of the big trees. That leaves the woods clear of trees. All that is left is young tree sprouts and plants."

"But if you cut down all the trees, there are no woods!" said Val.

Nate went on. "And there is even more. Without trees, the rain washes dirt away. This makes it hard for the forest to grow back. And the rivers get muddy, too."

"Oh, I heard about that," said Val. "It was on the news. More mud in the rivers is bad for the fish."

Nate had a grave look. "It gets worse," he said. "The law can be broken. In some places, most of the trees that are cut down should not be."

Val and Nate thought about the stumps they had seen. They wanted to find out if those trees should not have been cut. They knew that a mill was where cut trees were brought. Trees were sawed into boards at a mill. Then houses could be made with them.

The two searched the Web. They learned that there was a mill near school. It was called the Corte Mill. The Web site gave the mill's phone number.

Nate stood up. "We need to check this out,"

he said. "Let's see what we can find out at the mill."

Val wrote down the phone number. She told Nate she would call the mill.

CHAPTER 5

Knock on Wood

Val and Nate met Sam and Tess back in class.
Nate said they should walk to the Corte Mill
after school.

"Sounds good. Let me get the film stuff,"
said Val.

"I will carry it!" said Sam. Val rolled her
eyes, but she let Sam get it. Later, the group set
off walking to the mill. As they walked, a truck
pulled up next to them.

Looking over, the team saw the wood shop

teacher. Mr. Holz was going to the mill, too. He had to pick up wood for his class. Mr. Holz asked if they would like a ride.

"Sure," said Tess. The group got into the truck.

Soon they were at the mill. Large trucks with logs were parked there. The four friends went with Mr. Holz. He walked into a part of the mill. There, fresh cut boards were neatly stacked. A short man walked up to them.

"Hi, Mr. Holz," the man said. "Looks like you brought a film crew today!"

The teacher smiled. "Doug, this is a school group. They are here to learn about wood."

The man nodded. "Great! My name is

Doug. And it's good luck that you are here today."

"Why?" asked Tess, taking notes.

Doug leaned on a stack of boards. "Some think that standing close to wood or touching wood is good luck."

Mr. Holz rapped the wood with his hand. "Knock on wood," he said.

"Let me show you around," said Doug. First, the group had to put on glasses. These would keep their eyes safe. Then Doug took the group where the logs came off the trucks. There was a lot of noise and sawdust in the air. Val filmed as the huge logs were pulled off the trucks. From there, the logs were put on belts to go to the saws.

The team thought the saw blades would be round. But they were not like the saws they had seen before. These were band saw blades. The blades were on bands of steel. They were shaped like big rubber bands. At the end of each belt were many band saws. The log was pushed into the blades. Then many boards of wood came out the far end.

These boards were picked up. They were trimmed again with the next saw. These cuts made the boards all the same size. These boards would be dried. Then they would be sold.

"What is done with the tree bark and the sawdust?" asked Tess.

31

The log was pushed into the blades.

"We try to use every bit of the tree," said Doug. "A lot of our small wood scraps go to make cardboard. We crush the scraps into very small pieces. Huge stones do the crushing. Then we soak the pieces. The wood turns into pulp. Wood pulp can be shaped and dried into cardboard. Or into sheets like that," he said. He pointed to the pad that Tess was writing on. "One pine tree can make over 80,000 of those sheets."

Mr. Holz said, "Larger wood scraps can be used in my class. Doug lets me take them for free."

The team liked what they heard. Wood at the Corte Mill was not wasted.

Nate had been waiting to ask something. He turned to Doug. "Where does this mill get its trees?"

Doug said the trees came from loggers. Some loggers cut trees from their own land. Some logged on land where the law said it was OK.

Nate told Doug about the odd stumps he had seen with Val.

"It sounds like you should talk to someone at the park," said Doug.

The group got into Mr. Holz's truck. As they did, Sam saw that Tess had a small bag.

"What's that?" he asked. Tess said it was sawdust. It was for her pet mouse, Pip.

Sam laughed. "Tess, mice don't eat sawdust."

Now Tess laughed. "I know, Sam. But they do like to sleep in it."

CHAPTER 6

The Old Man of the Woods

The group took Doug's tip. Nate called the park on the phone. He spoke to a park worker named Kris. Nate told her about the film they were making. Kris said she would be glad to meet them. She would walk on the trails with them. Kris could talk to them about the trees and logging.

One week later, Nate, Sam, Tess, and Val were walking up a steep trail. Val was having a hard time. This was because she had to carry all the film stuff.

"Hey, you wanted to be in charge," Sam said.

After hiking for a mile, they saw Kris. She was waiting for them on a high ridge. From there, they could look out over many green treetops. The woods went as far as the eye could see.

"Wow!" said Tess. "I did not know this park was so big."

Nate told Kris that he liked being in the woods. He saw the park as a place where all living things could find peace.

Kris felt the same way. "My job is to keep trees and living things from being hurt. There are rare trees in this park. And some of them are 300 years old. They are called old growth trees."

Tess looked around. "Can loggers cut trees here?" she asked.

"Yes," said Kris. She pointed at a fallen tree on the trail. "But the loggers do not always cut living trees," said Kris. "Sometimes they take away trees that have been blown down by the wind."

"But loggers cut living trees too, right?" asked Nate. Kris tried to say something. Nate kept talking. "I think they might be cutting trees they should not! If they keep it up, there will be no park left."

"Kris wants to say something," said Tess.

Kris nodded again. "It is OK. Nate is partly right. Clear cutting is very bad. That is when all the trees in one spot are cut down. The soil washes away in the rain. The trees never grow back. That is why loggers can never clear cut in this park."

Val spoke up. "How do loggers know what trees to cut?"

"I tell them," said Kris. "I go into the woods. I mark the trees that can be logged."

Kris said that sometimes it was good for a tree to be taken away. With too much shade, young trees would not get the light they needed to grow. Some trees were sick or growing in spots where they might fall. A falling tree could hurt more trees on its way down. Kris said this kind of logging was good in two ways. One, it helped the other trees in the park. Two, the wood could be used to make houses.

"Take a close look around," said Kris. "You will see stumps here and there. Those were trees I marked for the loggers."

"Nate, those were the stumps we saw!" said Val.

Nate tried to take this in. "So the loggers only cut a few trees," he said. "And that helps the rest of the park." He could see that logging was not always a bad thing.

Kris pointed out a tree. It was one she

might mark to be cut by loggers. The tree was leaning far to the side. It looked like it could fall at any time. If it fell, it might knock down other trees or hurt people. Val made sure to get the leaning tree on film.

Kris then asked if they had time for a hike. She wanted to show them the oldest tree in the park. "Its name is the Old Man of the Woods. It is over 500 years old. We think it is the oldest tree of its kind in our state. Old Man is a pal I try to see each time I walk in the woods."

"As long as it's a short hike," said Val. "I have to get back to town by five."

"Why?" asked Nate.

"It has to do with wood," said Val. "I need

The tree was leaning far to the side.

to pick up my new skateboard."

Sam turned to Nate, Tess, and Kris. He spoke in a low voice. "I hope she takes better care of this one!"

"Hey, I heard that!" Val said. She handed the film stuff to Tess. And then she chased Sam down the trail.